John's Birthday Party

by Wes Magee
Illustrated by Marc Vyvyan-Jones

It's John's birthday party
and the whole family's there,
Mum and Dad,
sister Rachel
and Gran in her chair.

(**AND** one-eared Ted,
John's old moth-eaten bear.)

The two cats, Flip and Flop,
chase the dog, Bertie Beast,

while John's three crazy cousins

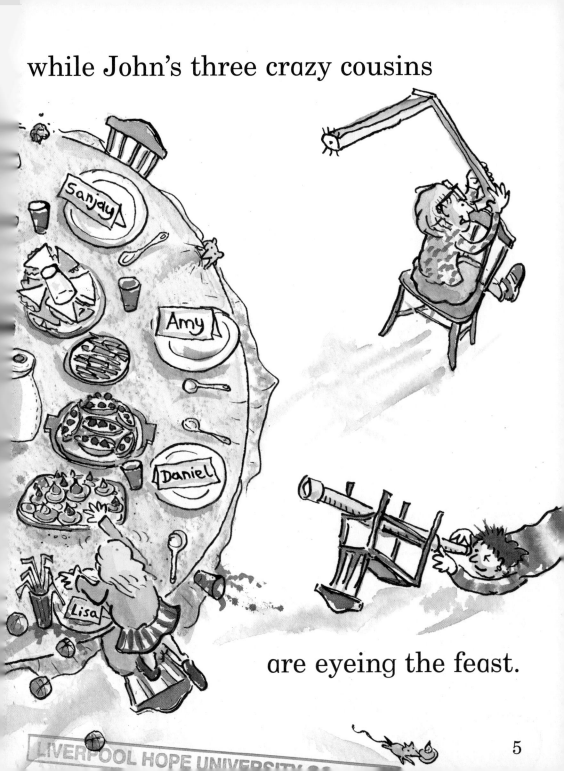

are eyeing the feast.

All the children dress up.
John asks,

"Who wins the prize?"

Dad says, "Superman Sam

... with his bug-monster eyes!"

Oh, there's a fantastic noise
and the laughter is hearty
when pets, girls and boys
are at John's birthday party.

WOOOOO!

(John's **big** birthday party.)

They play *Hide from the Ghost*.
"Wooooo! Wooooo!" they all shout.
Cousin Ella's the ghost.

"Sh ... sh ... she's coming!"

"Watch out!"

Some hide behind curtains.

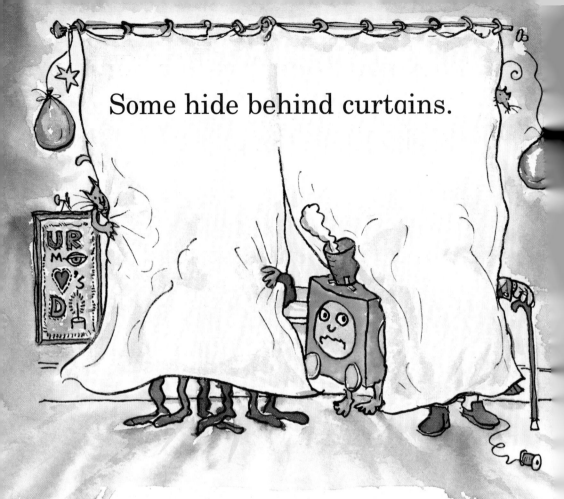

Some hide under chairs.

Mum says, "Sit down, you lot!

Now, play *Musical Box*."

"The next game," chortles John, "is

Burst the Balloons!"

Pets and children jump up

like a bunch of baboons.

Rachel catches the biggest

John

pop!

and then the whole gang

16

leap on the balloon
and it bursts with a

BANG!

Oh, there's a fantastic noise
and the laughter is hearty
when pets, girls and boys
are at John's birthday party.

choo!
choo!

(John's **great** birthday party.)

Mum says,
"Outside,
you
lot!

Let poor Gran have a snooze."

19

What a muddle of trainers

and red boots and shoes.

Dad is tearing his hair

and he's blowing a fuse.

In the tree house
John shows Sam and Ella his tricks.
He juggles with eggs …

... then he makes slime that sticks.

UGH!

"SPELLA-SMELLA!" shouts John

and he waves
his trick wand.

Down below ...

... Little Lisa falls into the pond.

SPLASH!

Mum says, "Okay, you lot,
time for John's birthday tea.
Who wants igloo ice cream?"

Here comes Dad with the cake.

"Stegosaurus!"

"Woweeeeeee!"

Faces shine. Candles glow.

Dad says, "Take a deep breath.
Ready?

One!

Two!

Three!

BLOW!"

What a WHOOSH!
What a SWOOSH!
The cake goes ... everywhere.

There's cake on the cats
and there's cake in Gran's hair!
(**AND** it's all over Ted,
John's old moth-eaten bear.)

Oh, there's a fantastic noise
and the laughter is hearty
when pets, girls and boys
are at John's birthday party.

(John's **best** birthday party.)

"A really cool party,"
says old one-eared Ted,
and he gives a good shake
of his moth-eaten head.